The BOY WITH TWO BELLY BUTTONS

By Stephen J. Dubner

Illustrated by Christoph Niemann

HarperCollins*Publishers*

Solomon never thought it was strange that he had
two belly buttons
until he got a baby sister.

Anya
only
had
one.

"She only has one belly button!" he told his parents. "We have to find the other one!"

"No," said his mother. "One is the right number of belly buttons."

The *right* number? So was something wrong with Solomon?

Solomon wanted to ask his parents some more questions about his belly buttons. But his parents were too busy with the new baby.

At the hospital, Solomon asked to speak with the person in charge of babies.

"I have two belly buttons," Solomon told her. "I would like to donate one of mine to any baby who doesn't have one."

The lady laughed. "I'm afraid all our babies already have a belly button."

"Let me check, my good friend."
Victor looked down at his belly.
"Seems like I have . . . **zero**.
Goodness. Why do you ask?"

"I have two. Would you like one?"

"Would I! Spectacular!"

Solomon hugged Victor.

"Just a moment," Victor said. "Why so generous?"
"Because I have two belly buttons and you have
zero," said Solomon. "And one is the right number."

"But—," began Solomon.
"I'm sorry," said Victor.
"Truly I am."

"The right number for *whom*?"
Victor sat down to think. "No,
no, this won't do. How can I be
the only turtle in town with a
belly button? That, my good
friend, is a recipe for ridicule."

Solomon went to the swimming pool, where he
looked around at all the tummies.
"What are *you* staring at?" said a teenage girl.
"Out of my way," said a hairy man.

One lady wore a bathing suit that covered her tummy. Solomon asked if he could peek inside it. "Where's your mommy?" she said.

Solomon never did see the lady's tummy. But all the other tummies were the same. They all had just one belly button.

Solomon went to the local college and found the professor
of buttonology.

"Excuse me," Solomon said. "What kind of buttons do you
study?"

"Well, let's see!" said the professor. "I study campaign
buttons, elevator buttons, Red Buttons, clothing buttons,
of course—"

"What about belly buttons?"

"Why, yes!" said the professor. "Innies, outies, pretzels,
corkscrews, and of course—"

"Have you ever seen anyone with *two* belly buttons?" Solomon asked. The professor blinked. "Two belly buttons? That is not possible!"
"Yes, it is," said Solomon.

"No, it is not!" said the professor. "Now run along home!"

Solomon began to cry. He was the only person in the whole world with two belly buttons.

Walking home, Solomon was so sad that he did not notice the hubbub at the movie theater.

There were bright lights and a red carpet. It was a premiere! A very famous movie director stood outside.

Solomon bumped right into him.

"Excuse me," Solomon said.

"That's okay," said the very famous movie director. He shook Solomon's hand. "How are you?"

"Not so good," Solomon said.

"What's wrong?" asked the director.

"Well," said Solomon, "have you ever heard of a boy with two belly buttons?"

The very famous movie director thought for a moment. "No," he said, "I haven't. But if there were such a boy, I sure would like to meet him. He'd have to be very special."

"Special?" Solomon said.
"Yes, special," said the director.

Solomon lifted up his shirt.
"Wow!" said the very famous movie
director. "Can I make a movie about you?"

"Do you make good
movies?" Solomon said.

"Yes, I do," said the director.
"Let me think it over," Solomon said.
He took the very famous movie
director's card and went home.

Before he went to sleep, Solomon
looked at his tummy in the mirror.
For the first time in a long time,
he liked what he saw.

For Solomon (the real one) and Anya,
the most precious rascals alive
—S.J.D.

The Boy with Two Belly Buttons
Text copyright © 2007 by Stephen J. Dubner
Illustrations copyright © 2007 by Christoph Niemann

Printed in the U.S.A.

Library of Congress Cataloging-in-Publication Data is available.
ISBN-10: 0-06-113402-3 (trade bdg.) – ISBN-13: 978-0-06-113402-9 (trade bdg.)
ISBN-10: 0-06-113403-1 (lib. bdg.) – ISBN-13: 978-0-06-113403-6 (lib. bdg.)

Designed by Stephanie Bart-Horvath
2 3 4 5 6 7 8 9 10
❖
First Edition